# MIKEY

by Mindee Pinto +
Judy Cohen

Published by Orange Hat Publishing 2013

ISBN 978-1-937165-41-3

Printed in the United States of America

This book is a work of fiction. All names, characters, places, and incidents are products of the author's imagination. Any resemblance to actual events, locations, or persons (living or dead) is entirely coincidental.

www.orangehatpublishing.com

# PREFACE

The population of children diagnosed with autism increases on a yearly basis in many public and private school systems, but many classrooms are not getting better at understanding children with autism.

In this book, Mikey explains how a young child with autism sees, hears, and feels the world around him in his school environment.

*Mikey* is not just intended for educators; although, all teachers should read it to their classes. It is intended to educate adults as well as young children to increase their awareness and understanding of the child with autism. This book, and others to follow, was inspired by my vast experiences as a teacher working with children with autism.

Acknowledgments:

My gratitude extends to my mother, my co-author and incredible teacher; my husband, who is and will forever be my rock and support; my father, who supported us all with his encouragement to go forward; and to Mark and Margaret Fairbanks, for their honest, compassionate, and incredible vision.

Thanks to Mikey,
Mindee Pinto

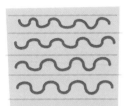

**WELCOME!**

Today is Mikey's first day of school.

Teachers would call the sounds coming from the classroom "exciting" and "fun."

Mikey sees it as "too much."

Mikey might cry, he might scream, he might even flap his hands when he hears the noises.

The noises might even make Mikey want to run from the room.

We want Mikey to feel happy every day.

"Hi, I'm Mikey.

This is my first day at school."

WHIRRRRRRRRRRRRRR

There are so many new
faces and sounds and
colors on the wall.

I see pictures hanging
from the ceiling.

These things scare me.

*I hear people saying, "Hi, Mikey, come on in, sit down."*

*I don't know what to do. I want to scream and run away.*

*I hope these new faces don't think I am being bad or mean; this is just me.*

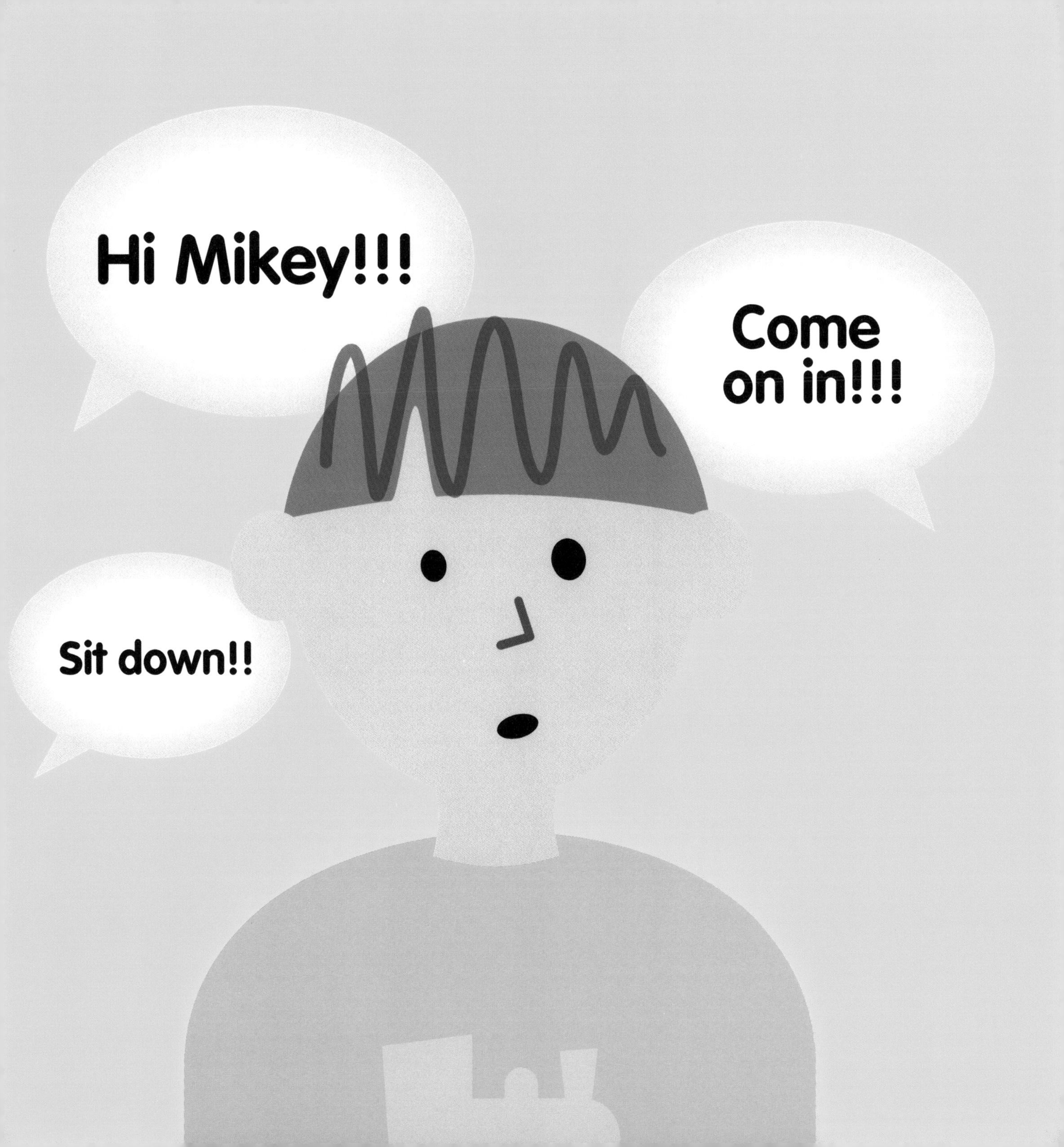
Hi Mikey!!!
Come on in!!!
Sit down!!

At school there are lots of noises.

It doesn't seem to bother the other children.
But to Mikey, it is very loud.

The lights make noise; they buzz.

The furnace makes noise; it hums.

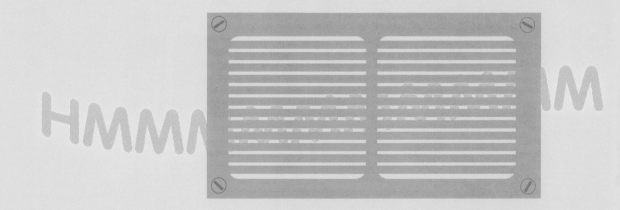

RRRRRRIIIIIINNNNNGGGGG

The bell makes noise; it rings.

And the children make noise; they laugh and talk.

These noises can hurt Mikey's ears.

YOU'RE IT!!! WOO-HOO!!

He might cover his ears with his hands,
and when he does, he may look different.

Mikey may want to wear headphones,
and that is okay.

We want Mikey to feel happy every day.

It is too loud in here.

*It looks like all these new faces are happy.*

*I am happy too, when it is not so noisy.*

I may have to cover my ears to make the noises stop.

BUZZZZBUZZZZBUZZZZBUZZZZBUZZZZBUZZZZ

YOU'RE IT!!! WOO-HOO!!

RRRRRIIIIINNNNGGGG

HA!!!

READY OR NOT HEAR I C

HMMMMMMMM

Covering my ears makes me feel better.

It's time to do an art project.

We love the feeling of shaving cream, cotton balls, sand,
and finger paint.

Why doesn't Mikey want to touch them?

He likes to say "no" when the teacher wants him to do the art project; he might even cry.

These things do not feel good on Mikey's hands.

Mikey does not want to sit at the art table with us.

That is okay. Tomorrow he might like art time.

We want Mikey to feel happy every day.

I like art time, but I don't like to touch all that messy "stuff."

I feel like crying when the teacher makes me feel the gooey, squishy "stuff."

*I want to be like the smiling faces, but I can't.*
*Maybe tomorrow I will like art time.*

When our teacher tells us what to do and where to go,
we listen and do it.

Mikey needs pictures to help him do what the teacher asks.

It's okay to have pictures.

We want Mikey to be happy every day.

I like pictures.

Pictures help me understand what I need to do and where I need to go.

Sometimes I don't understand all the words I hear.

I understand the pictures, and it makes me feel happy.

Sometimes Mikey stands too close when he says "hi" to us.

We have to tell him, "Stand back, Mikey" or "Not so close, Mikey." At first it was scary. But now we know that it is Mikey's way of being a friend.

We want Mikey to be happy every day.

I like saying "hi" to my friends.

I like it when they say "hi" back to me.

I like to look very closely at their faces.

I don't mean to get so close and make them mad.

It is just my way of saying "hi" and being a friend.

Tonight at 9...
Tonight at 9...
Tonight at 9...
Tonight at 9...
Tonight at 9...

Sometimes when Mikey talks, he says the same words over and over and over.

Sometimes he makes noises over and over and over.

Even when we tell him to stop, he keeps saying the same words.

He is not trying to be mean; he just can't stop.

Stopping may take him awhile, and that's okay.

We want Mikey to be happy every day.

When I feel upset or scared, I like to talk a lot about the same thing.

Sometimes it makes my teacher and some of the new faces angry.

I don't want to make anyone angry.

I just can't help it; talking makes me feel better.

When I feel better, my talking may stop.

Paper clip

Paper clip!

Paper clip!

Paper clip!

Paper clip!

Paper clip!

Mikey is our friend.

He may not act like we do, but we want Mikey to be happy in school every day.

I like my friends at school, and I know my friends like me too.
I want to be happy at school. I want my friends to be happy too.

CPSIA information can be obtained
at www.ICGtesting.com
Printed in the USA
LVIW020324240413
330668LV00002B